I0619604

# MOUNTAIN HUSBAND

## A CURVY GIRL/AGE GAP ROMANCE

### MOUNTAIN MEN OF HIGH RIDGE
### BOOK ONE

## HALLIE BENNETT

THE
ARROWED
HEART

 Formatted with Vellum

**Every Hallie Bennett book features a curvy girl & a filthy-talking hero!**

# DESCRIPTION

**SECURITY IS ALL SHE WANTS.**

With a history of absent parents and a younger sister bent on getting in trouble, responsible eldest daughter, Davie Overland, lives a safe and cautious life.

*Until custody of her baby nephew is threatened, and Davie must find his biological father—her sister's former one-night stand—before it's too late.*

**FAMILY IS ALL HE CRAVES.**

Gruff Cormac Madsen is busy saving his family's ranch from ruin. His dad left behind a mess, and despite help from his brother Connor, ranch life doesn't leave much time for love.

*Until a curvy woman appears on his land with a shocking announcement, and Cormac's dreams of a family might be closer than he thinks.*

# 1

## DAVIE OVERLAND

"His name was Mac," my sister says from the other side of the glass in Gumbrush County Women's Penitentiary.

"That's it? No last name?" I drop my phone on my lap. Forget about taking notes of details from the night she got pregnant with my nephew, Jesse. All she remembers is a freaking name.

"Sorry." She shrugs. Her orange jumpsuit wrinkles at the shoulders, another reminder of where we are, and I hate that our lives have come to this.

My little sister was charged for driving under the influence and will be stuck behind bars for the next two years, thanks to her prior arrests.

Then, there's me.

The responsible older sister who tried to keep her on the straight and narrow, failed, and is now responsible for raising her eight-month-old baby.

*If* I can find this mysterious man in High Ridge that Jessica claims is the biological father.

Not her on-again/off-again ex-boyfriend, Cody, who makes me uncomfortable every time I see him.

Which, unfortunately, has been a lot lately, since Jessica got locked up.

She and Jesse had been living with me, making me the natural choice as my nephew's guardian, but Cody and his mom have been causing trouble.

Protesting my custody.

*For the welfare checks*, according to Jessica.

That's why she finally admitted that Cody may not be Jesse's real dad, because she slept with one other guy around the time she got pregnant. Some stranger at a High Ridge bar after she stopped there on the drive home from visiting a friend out of town.

Now I have to find Mac, convince him that taking a court-mandated paternity test won't ruin his life because I'm willing to care for Jesse, and then pray this man isn't worse than Cody.

The judge granted me temporary custody of my nephew to allow for the paternity tests to be taken. Otherwise, Jesse would probably already be in Cody's possession.

We drew the short straw when it came to judges because ours has a bias against single women raising kids and almost always sides with the bio parents, especially dads.

But I can't let Jesse go to Cody and his mom. They've barely been in his life, and Cody is just as mixed up in drugs as my sister.

Based on what I've heard from Jessica and seen for myself on the court steps, his mom isn't much better.

"Okay, Mac from High Ridge. You met at a bar some time last in October. Great..." This feels like trying to find a needle in a haystack. "Wish me luck!"

A wary smile trembles to the forefront before I wave goodbye and start the awkward process of backtracking through prison security. My best friend is babysitting Jesse for me, so that's where I head, mentally preparing myself for our trip tomorrow.

Seven hours of driving.

Seven hours of agonizing over what awaits us in High Ridge, Washington.

Will we find Jesse's bio dad?

I don't have much of a plan outside of asking around town if anyone knows a Mac, and that's flimsy as fuck.

He could have been passing through, just like my sister, but I've got to try.

For Jesse.

He deserves a chance with a loving and stable father. Barring that, I'll settle for a man who will happily agree to give me custody.

A billboard for the pediatric hospital passes overhead.

*We're here for your family.*

A smiling baby looks over his mom's shoulder on the giant advertisement, and it hits me that the cheesy line could be my motto.

Because I'm the one who is always there for my family.

Our dad disappeared when I was four and Jessica was a newborn, and our mom is distant most of the time. Except when she needs a daughter to show off, and I'm the one she calls.

And hell, I practically raised Jessica.

A self-deprecating snort bursts free. "Look how well that turned out."

Jessica is a mess.

A convicted felon.

An addict.

*No wonder that judge is hesitant about me raising Jesse.*

The pessimistic thought does nothing for the nerves forming a sickly black pit in my stomach. It only adds to the pressure for tomorrow's trip to be a success.

I can't afford to fail my nephew like I did my sister.

I have to find this Mac.

He's my only hope.

# 2

## CORMAC MADSEN

Exhaustion weighs on my chest like a thousand-pound horse as the shrill bleat of my alarm signals another early start to a busy day. I sigh then roll into a sitting position.

"Fuck!" I snarl beneath my breath as my grandmother's old quilt falls to my waist, baring my naked chest to the 5 A.M. chill.

We're at the tail end of winter, which means the weather will soon change and bring with it an uptick in corporate retreats—part of a model the ranch shifted to after my dad died three years ago.

To remain profitable, and prevent the Rocking M from falling into disrepair like a lot of surrounding ranches, we transitioned from a true cattle ranch located at the base of Black Mountain to a rustic playground for wealthy guests.

It was my younger brother Connor's idea, since he's in charge of the ranch's finances, and so far, his business plan is working, but that doesn't mean I love the necessary decision.

Scrubbing a hand over my tired eyes, I stand and groan at the slight ache in my back. *Jesus.* Sometimes I feel a century older than my forty-three years.

And it's not just because my job is physically taxing. I'm used to hard work; it's been my constant since I was old enough to follow Dad around the Rocking M.

No, it's more than the routine of the ranch.

"It's my fucking life," I say aloud to an empty bathroom suite. The sparse counter and shower shelving perfectly illustrate my point as water spits from the showerhead.

Despite the two-sink vanity and oversized walk-in shower, it's obvious only one person uses the space. Two-in-one shampoo and conditioner. Bar soap and washcloth.

Utilitarian and lacking a woman's touch.

*Like me.*

I can't remember the last time I've felt anything more intimate than a handshake or brief man-hug from my brother or best friends.

At this rate, I'm going to die grizzled and alone after a lifetime of manual labor. No woman to call my own. No kids to teach about the ranch like my father taught me.

"Shit... It's too early to be this maudlin." But more and more lately, it's been difficult to stop my thoughts from straying toward a pathetic future barreling at me.

Buttoning a flannel shirt over a white tee after my shower, I head downstairs where the smell of breakfast hangs in the air.

"Morning, Fancy," I say as I walk straight for the pot of coffee on the counter.

"Good morning! Everything's laid out in the dining room. Connor and Deacon are already there." Fancy uses her spatula to point toward the other room then flips another flapjack on the griddle.

Sixty-three and spry as ever, she used to own her name-sake, Fancy's Diner, in downtown High Ridge—otherwise known as Main Street like every other small town in America. Officially, Fancy retired years ago after leaving the diner to her niece, but retirement got boring real fast, apparently.

So, when the Rocking M began searching for a chef to cater meals to ranch staff and guests, she'd offered her services, and I'd happily accepted the help.

"Look who finally decided to grace us with his presence." Connor grins from his seat at the head of the table.

"Let's switch places, and we'll see how fast you move," I retort, sitting beside Deacon with a plate full of eggs, bacon, and Fancy's flapjacks.

When Dad died, he left the ranch to both of his sons in an even split. Fifty-percent to my younger brother. Fifty-percent to me. It just so happens that my share encompasses more of the manual labor required to keep things running, while Connor's focuses on the financial side of the setup.

Not that I begrudge our roles. Connor is a whiz with numbers, and he's used his business school contacts to grow Rocking M's reputation as the perfect place for a corporate retreat.

"Sitting behind a desk all day has made him soft." Connor scoffs at Deacon's bemused assessment.

Patting his flat stomach, my brother shakes his head in denial. "Lies. Your old age is showing Deac if you've already forgotten how I helped you with those barn roof repairs yesterday."

The two devolve into a duel of playful barbs—similar to almost every other day at meals—and again, my thoughts drift toward a different kind of life.

One where the dining table is fuller.

One where my dream girl is cozied into my side, sharing my amusement at Connor and Deacon's antics, while our children chirp from the sidelines.

One big, happy family.

*And a fucking pipe dream.*

# 3
## DAVIE

Linnea and I arrived in High Ridge late in the afternoon, exhausted and a little hangry, after our seven-hour drive extended into ten hours, thanks to Jesse.

The little man protested each hour locked in his car seat with crying tantrums, diaper blowouts, and an episode of projectile vomit onto the passenger headrest. Linnea had taken it in stride, despite needing to spot wash her hair at a grungy truck stop.

By the time we'd checked in at Timber Bed and Breakfast, we'd agreed that our search for the mysterious Mac could wait until the next day, allowing us time to recover from the stress-filled journey.

But as the morning sun beams through the window, I wish I could pull the covers back over my head and ignore the fact that today the search for Jesse's bio dad officially begins.

Noise from the bathroom alerts me to Linnea's presence, her double bed next to mine empty and rumpled.

"Guess that means I can't stall any longer." I sigh and

turn my head, quietly watching Jesse through the mesh netting of his travel crib. Judging by the bright light and Linnea's activity, I doubt he'll sleep much longer, but it's comforting to see him so peaceful.

He has no idea the upheaval potentially coming his way. All he knows is the warm safety of his small crib and favorite stuffed giraffe.

A few rogue tears slip from the corner of my eye. I haven't felt that safe and secure in a long time, probably not since I was Jesse's age.

Back when our father was still around—two parents, food on the table, and a roof over our heads. A thread of tension twined around every aspect of our lives, though, and it only got worse after he left. We lived paycheck to paycheck, while a steady stream of Mom's boyfriends came in and out of our lives.

Linnea exits the bathroom and notices I'm awake. "Ready to find your sister's baby daddy?" she jokes, trying to lighten the mood.

Covertly swiping at my damp cheek, I sit up and lean against the headboard. "Ready as I'll ever be. The bar opens at four, so I'm not optimistic about our chances until then, but maybe we'll get lucky."

"Fingers crossed." She raises two hands with crossed fingers to double our luck, and I smile, thankful she offered to join me on this trip as moral support.

We've been friends for over a decade, and she's the only one who knows my entire family history. Who understands the turmoil I've gone through with Jessica, even before she got pregnant.

"Let me change and brush my teeth, then we can check out Fancy's Diner across the street for breakfast and, hope-fully, some intel."

A half hour later, Linnea, Jesse, and I are seated by a window overlooking Main Street while a waitress puts in our order of pancakes, eggs, and bacon after admitting she doesn't know a Mac.

Blue gingham tablecloths and chair cushions decorate the cozy cafe, and the matching pattern bordering the walls ties everything together.

It's cute and rustic, and in any other situation, the easy comfort of such a quaint diner would bring peace of mind. Like I'm drinking Hallmark happiness straight from the source.

Unfortunately, the rest of the town is a little too rundown to embody the same vibe.

"So, how do you want to do this?" Linnea asks.

I spoon mushed bananas into Jesse's gaping mouth and think for a second.

"It'll probably be faster to split up, if you're okay with going alone. We each take one side of Main Street and work our way down the open storefronts."

"Sounds like a plan."

We finish eating, then Linnea and I split outside on the sidewalk. Jesse's happy babble emanates from his secure place in the stroller. Like this is any other day where we enjoy a walk in the sun and fresh air.

"Come on, little man. Let's find your dad."

First, we stop in the antique store next to the cafe. The older woman behind the counter is kind but ultimately no help.

The same goes for the florist, the pharmacy, and a shoe store.

Linnea and I are making quick work of the small-town shops, but I'm losing hope that we'll find someone who knows the man we're looking for.

I'm about to give up and wait for the only bar on Main Street to open up when the last building on the block is all that's left to canvas. The scent of wood dust and paint thinner wrinkles my nose as I enter the hardware store.

"Morning! How can I help you?" A middle-aged man approaches us with a friendly smile. His red polo has the name 'Greg' stitched on the chest in white.

I swallow the lump in my throat and launch into the spiel I've repeated multiple times this morning.

"Hi, I'm hoping you can help me find someone. I don't have much to go on, but his name is Mac."

Greg's eager steps stutter to a halt once he realizes I'm not a customer, and his smile transforms into a quizzical frown.

"Mac?"

"Yes... Do you know anybody around here who goes by that?" I shrug, feeling another disheartening *no* about to come my way. "It might be a nickname? Short for something else? Or a last name?"

My voice gets smaller and smaller with each suggestion as Greg mulls over the possibilities. None of them appear to light a bulb of recognition above his head.

"Sorry, I don't think—"

"Did you say Mac? Like Cormac Madsen over at Rocking M Ranch?" The newcomer towers over me and Greg, a black baseball cap with an O'Hare Salvage logo doing nothing to disguise his considerable height.

"Maybe? Like I told him," I gesture to Greg. "I don't know much more than his name, or part of it, anyway."

The man scratches his bearded cheek with his thumb as his curious gaze sweeps over me and the stroller holding a napping Jesse.

"The thing is," he drawls, "Cormac only uses Mac with...

out-of-towners." The way he delicately says the word makes it obvious he's being discreet, but I don't have time to be polite.

My sister had a one-night stand that resulted in an accidental pregnancy.

I'm way past the point of needing my delicate sensibilities protected.

"You mean flings," I say flatly. "He uses a nickname with women he doesn't plan on seeing again."

Both men have the decency to flush red at my bald assessment.

"Yes, ma'am."

"And where did you say he worked? A ranch?"

"The Rocking M. It's situated just outside town proper to the west," Greg provides, proving somewhat useful, despite being unfamiliar with *Cormac*.

"Thank you. Both of you." My hand lifts in farewell before I wheel Jesse through the glass entry door, which Greg hurries to open for us. "Thanks," I mutter, already reaching for my phone to text Linnea about this lead.

But I don't get very far because she's already crossing the street to meet us. Two iced coffees fill her hands, until she gives one to me, so she can shield her face from the sun.

"I've got a name and location," I say before slurping a mouthful of caffeine and sugar.

"Cormac Madsen at Rocking M Ranch," Linnea blurts before I've even had a chance to swallow.

"How'd you know?"

"A lady at the coffee shop said he might be our Mac. That's why I was coming to see you guys. To tell you the good news."

"*Potentially* good news," I stress, steering the stroller

back toward the B&B down the street. "Did she mention how he only goes by Mac with one-night stands?"

Linnea chokes on her iced coffee and pounds on her chest to clear her airway. "No! Seriously?"

"That's what the guy at the hardware store said." At the B&B, we wave hello to the receptionist then board the elevator before continuing our conversation.

"No wonder Jessica didn't have many details to share. He purposely kept it that way." Each floor button lights up until we reach the third level. "Not that Jessica was probably any better."

"This is when experience with casual sex would be helpful," Linnea says right as the doors open to reveal an older couple gaping at us. The woman clutches the pearls hanging around her neck—*yes, actual pearls*—while her husband frowns in disapproval.

Stifling a laugh, we hurry past them, quickly unlock the door to our shared room, then let the giggles free.

"Oh my god, I can't believe you said that," I gasp, holding my side as more laughter bubbles up.

"We were both thinking it."

She's not wrong.

If Jessica is the wild younger sister who doesn't balk at sex with strangers, I'm the eldest sibling who would never consider hopping into bed with someone unless I've known them for... well, let's just say a *long* time.

So long that I haven't figured out the timeline yet, because I'm technically still a virgin—self-made, battery-operated orgasms aside.

After witnessing my mom's relationships, then suffering through Jessica following in her footsteps, I've vowed not to put myself in such a risky situation.

I need stability. Security. Safety. A serious *relationship*.

It's just my luck that those items are hard to come by these days.

My breaths slowly even out as my amusement fades, and reality sets in. I've got a lead, which means it's up to me to check it out.

Grabbing my purse from the mesh basket beneath Jesse's stroller, I straighten with determination. "Will you be okay watching Jesse while I verify Cormac is our Mac?"

"I'll be fine, but are you sure you want to go alone?"

"No, but I don't want to drive out there with Jesse yet, and we can't leave him here by himself."

Linnea sighs and nods in agreement. As much as I'd love to have backup while meeting a stranger, who may become a permanent fixture in my life if it turns out he really is Jesse's dad, I have to do this alone.

Another snort of amusement threatens at the realization, though, this time it's tinged with bitterness.

Solving problems by myself isn't new.

I'm a master at going it alone, and meeting Mr. Cormac Madsen won't be any different.

# 4

## CORMAC

Sweat drips into my eyes as I tighten the fencing on the east side of Rocking M Ranch. The red bandana stuffed in the back of my Levi's has seen better days, but it does the job, mopping my brow and the back of my neck before I shove it into my pocket again.

My horse nickers in greeting as the sound of pounding hooves nears. Setting my tools aside, I rise to my feet, blinking against the sun cutting beneath my hat.

"Got an issue, boss," my foreman and one of my best friends says with a tip of his chin. "Garrett never fixed that broken post where the herd is grazing. One of the heifers got spooked, tried to jump the fence, and got scraped all to hell. The vet's on his way now."

"Goddammit!" Removing my leather gloves, I gather the manual auger and shovel and pack them away before mounting Rollo, a sorrel Quarter horse who's been my dependable companion for the past decade. "Where's Garrett now?"

"I radioed the stables about twenty minutes ago once I

discovered the injured heifer. He was last seen shooting the shit with Hank and Clyde by the goat pen."

Gritting my teeth, I turn Rollo in that direction with Deacon close behind. Swaying grass stretches toward the mountains to the north of us, a spectrum of changing colors as spring battles winter for supremacy.

This is our busy season. The beginning of spring retreats and summer vacations. And how are we going to start it? Short-handed because Garrett can't follow simple fucking directions.

I hired him as a favor to his uncle. He's young and inexperienced, but I can work with those things. There's nothing wrong with starting from scratch and learning as you go. Training ranch hands is practically my second job.

What I can't fix is a bad attitude.

Something Garrett has in spades.

He balks at authority. Sneers at constructive criticism. Honestly, if Buck Headly wasn't his uncle, and a good neighbor, I would have kicked Garrett's ass off my property months ago.

Like his first fucking day here.

Instead, I gave him chance after chance to improve, but my tolerance for his bullshit has finally reached its end.

When one of mine gets hurt? Whether it's a thousand-pound heifer, a barn kitten, or one of my employees, I don't take that shit lightly.

The main house, barn, stables, and various animal pens come into view, and sure enough, there is Garrett's wiry length lazing against a wooden post, jawing with two other ranch hands.

Grinning like he doesn't have a care in the world.

Motherfucker.

I ride right up to the trio before hopping to the ground with a heavy thump.

"Garrett!" I shout, the anger dammed in my veins exploding into action. The younger man startles and straightens. "You're fucking fired!"

"'You can't—"

He doesn't have a chance to finish his snide retort before my fist flies into his jaw with a bone-breaking crack.

But it's not the satisfying howl of pain from Garrett that snags my attention. It's the high-pitched squeak of fear. A feminine gasp of shock that is out of place on a ranch full of men.

Following the sound, my eyes whip across the dirt between the main house and goat pen until they land on a sweet little brunette who's slowly retreating to a gray sedan.

A gust of wind tosses her hair across her cheeks and causes the loose sweater that falls midthigh to mold to her lush breasts and round belly.

*Fuck, who the hell is she?*

The woman is a tempting sight, especially for a man who spends most of his time alone, but I can imagine what she sees when she looks at me.

A violent beast with no self-control.

# 5
## DAVIE

*Please don't be him.*

*Please don't be Cormac.*

When no one answered the door at the house, I wandered off the porch steps and headed toward a group of men standing by a pen full of goats. My gaze drifted over each man as if one would magically glow with the words, *I slept with your sister and fathered your nephew.*

Of course, none of them had a tell-tale sign that he was the man I was looking for.

The entire drive here I sifted through explanations and questions, searching for the best way to broach the topic of *Hey, you might be a daddy... congratulations!* But words deserted me the closer I got to the men.

Except it didn't matter.

Because a bullish man stormed into the yard, thunder roaring in his wake, before he shouted, "Garrett!" then punched one of the guys in the jaw.

My cry of fear broke the sudden silence, and all eyes turned on me—including the dark gaze of the man emanating fearsome authority and brutality—rather than the bleeding man hunched over in the dirt.

This isn't right.

I shouldn't be here.

I can't bring my nephew, *a baby*, here. It's not safe. I'll have to figure out another way to keep him out of Cody's greedy clutches.

My gaze remains locked on the dangerous stranger as I slowly retreat. Like a predator's soft, squishy prey, instinct tells me not to run. Not to turn my back on this man.

Fumbling behind my back, the cool metal of my car's door handle greets my fingertips, and a breath of relief stutters from my chest.

Or tries to.

It gets stuck in my throat once I register that my escape won't be so easy.

Because that man is stalking forward. His boots kick up dust clouds of warning; his reddened knuckles flex at his side as if itching to do more harm.

Or to capture an errant visitor.

*Me.*

"Who are you?" he asks, the low boom of his voice sliding across my nerves to prod them into full-blown panic.

"N-No one. I m-made a wrong turn and..." I flinch when he lifts his hand, and immediately, he stops his advance.

"I'm not going to hurt you." This time, both his hands raise slightly as if he's trying to calm a wild horse. "I'm sorry for scaring you. It's bad luck you were here to witness my blow-up; usually, I'm more professional."

"You mean you don't go around hitting coworkers for no reason?"

"Ex-employee," he corrects. "And not for no reason.

Thanks to him not doing his job properly, one of the animals was injured."

"Oh."

"Is everything okay?" Another man joins us, his sharp features similar to the one in front of me. "I heard yelling then a scream."

"Everything's fine, Connor. I fired Garrett. Can you escort him off the property?"

Curiosity fills the air, but Connor doesn't press the issue. He spins on his heel to presumably follow instructions from his boss.

"Now, why don't you tell me what you're really doing here, sweetheart? Because I doubt a wrong turn took you down my two-mile drive. Most folks course correct at the gravel turnout a hundred yards down the road."

*Shit.* I recall the wide patch of rocks he's talking about, because I *did* consider making a U-turn and coming up with a different plan for keeping custody of Jesse.

My tensed shoulders slouch at being caught in a lie, and only years of rallying my courage prompts me to speak the truth.

"My name is Davie Overland. My sister is Jessica Overland." No recognition on his face at the name. "Last May, a man met a woman at a bar for a one-night stand; that was my sister. I'm here today because she thinks that man might be the biological father of her eight-month-old son. I've come to ask him to take a paternity test. It's technically court-mandated, but since we didn't know his last name or address..."

"How'd that lead you here to my ranch?" The question should come off as accusatory, but surprisingly, his tone remains even. Like he's processing the news that he or someone he employs might be a dad before jumping to a swift denial.

*Thank god.*

After witnessing his fury with Garrett, it wouldn't have shocked me to have his ire turned on me.

"I asked around Main Street. All Jessica remembered was the name Mac and High Ridge. Someone at the hardware store thought a guy named Cormac might go by Mac," I explain, wringing my sweaty hands together. "This is the Rocking M Ranch, right?"

"It is, and I'm Cormac Madsen, the owner."

*Double shit.*

It's him.

The man who punches his employees, or recently fired ones, might be Jesse's dad.

He motions to the house. "Let's go inside and sort this out. I don't need the whole ranch listening to my business."

"Uh... Of course." I don't blame him for wanting to keep this private, but I'm not thrilled about being alone with him in his house.

*You'll be fine. We're surrounded by ranch workers, and Linnea knows where you're at.*

If Cormac could be trusted, he had a legitimate reason for flying off the handle. I'd be pissed, too, if someone hurt an animal, but that doesn't negate the fact that his first choice was to punch a man.

Thankfully, Mom's revolving door of loser boyfriends never included the violent type, but I'm still wary. Neither Mom nor Jessica have great track records with men.

Even if Cormac barely qualifies as one of Jessica's men, I can't imagine he varies much from her usual type—untrustworthy and skeevy.

Okay, so Cormac doesn't seem skeevy.

Honestly, if my first impression wasn't of him beating up a man, I'd probably find him attractive with his silver-flecked hair and beard. Those piercing brown eyes narrowed with lines of maturity at the edges.

Too bad his temper concerns me.

*Oh, yeah... and he fucked my sister.*

# 6

## CORMAC

Today is turning into one hell of a shit show.

First, Garrett's reckless behavior, and now, *this*. I might be a fucking dad. To a baby born to a woman I have no memory of.

I'd be the first to admit that I'm not exactly a monk. I have sex often enough, but for the life of me, I don't recall Jessica.

However, it doesn't surprise me that if we fucked in October, I don't remember her. It was probably during one of my drunk evenings at the bar on the weekend of the anniversary of my dad's death.

It's been three years since he's been gone, and each year, I drown myself in a bottle of whiskey. Partly to numb the pain, but also to ignore the guilt I feel over his death.

He left too soon, leaving a ranch behind that has been a struggle to make profitable, hence the much-needed shift to its current stint as a dude ranch.

So, if what Davie says is true, I very well could have met her sister on one of those drunken nights and gotten her pregnant.

I open the door to the house and wave Davie through to the sitting room.

"Why don't you tell me the full story? What's this about the courts?" I ask, bracing myself in a leather chair by the fireplace while she sits on the edge of a loveseat my momma adored.

"Where to start?" She offers a half-grin and licks her lips nervously.

My gaze drops to the wet gleam on soft, rosy pink before dragging my eyes somewhere safer, like the windowpane behind her head.

"Jessica has always been a wild child. She does what she wants when she wants, and unfortunately, that means drinking too much and experimenting with drugs. She also tends to gravitate towards people that enjoy the same things, like her ex-boyfriend Cody."

Davie tucks a strand of hair behind her ear, though it immediately pops free. She swipes at it again, and this time I notice the slight tremble of her fingers.

She's nervous and scared, and I wish I knew how much of her fear was because of me and how much was due to our situation.

Because the last thing I want is for this woman to be afraid of me.

*Why? So, you can fuck her, too?*

*That's never happening, especially if you fathered a son with her sister.*

"Cody and Jessica were on a break when she passed through High Ridge. I can't say for certain if that truly would have mattered—whether she was in a relationship or not when she met you—or if things wouldn't have happened the same, but that's what she told me."

Another deep breath, then she continues.

"She found out she was pregnant ten weeks later. I'm guessing that her *extracurriculars* messed with her birth control." Davie shrugs after using air quotes around *extracurriculars*, clearly referring to Jessica's drug use. "Either way, she moved in with me so I'd be able to take care of her during the pregnancy and the baby when he came. He's eight months old."

"His name is Jesse. After her." She rolls her eyes toward the ceiling. "I assumed Cody was the dad, and she let Cody believe that, although she's never officially confirmed it. He actually hasn't been in Jesse's life very much because they haven't been together in a while. But a month ago, Jessica got pulled over for driving under the influence, and now she's serving time for the next two years, which means Jesse needs a guardian."

My brows furrow. "You don't qualify?"

A flash of annoyance erases some of her discomfiture before she explains, "Cody decided he wanted to protest my custody. Jessica assumes it's for the welfare money. That's why she finally told me that Cody may not be the dad."

"And that's where I come in," I say, sorting through everything she shared.

"Right. The judge ordered a paternity test to be taken by you and Cody. If Cody is the biological father, I'm worried the judge will side with him. I guess he has a thing against single women, and likes to keep children with their biological parents, especially dads. It would not be safe for Jesse to be with Cody and his mom," she stresses. "So, I'm really hoping that you are his dad. We're not expecting much, just for you to agree to me having custody."

"Whoa, whoa, whoa." I stop her with a wave of my hand.

There's a knot in my gut at the knowledge that I might

have had a kid the past eight months and not known it, but the idea of ignoring a child once confirming his paternity is a hard fucking no.

"If he's my son, I'm not going to abandon him."

"You can't expect me to leave my nephew with a stranger," she says, wringing her hands until the knuckles turn white. "The judge would probably approve, but—"

"What if we give the judge exactly what he wants and strengthen our case against this Cody guy? In case he tries to claim parental rights, since he's been around since the baby's birth."

A crazy idea takes shape in my mind as the words spill free. I'm not prone to spontaneous decisions, but Davie and my potential baby have decimated the past, responsible Cormac.

Current me is hungry for what Davie is offering… and willing to bargain for what she's not.

"What do you mean?" she asks.

"Well, if I'm the biological dad, and you're the biological aunt, wouldn't that mean our case is stronger together versus a parent who doesn't share any DNA with Jesse?"

"I guess so, but I'm still not following."

"We get married," I say, leaning forward and catching a whiff of her sweet magnolia scent. "Legally, Jesse would be both of ours. You'd still be with him, and Cody wouldn't have a leg to stand on."

Davie sits stunned and silent for a moment. A range of emotions crash over her round features before landing on utter astonishment.

"You want to get married? I don't even know you… A-And you slept with my sister!"

"Who I don't even remember." The admission sounds callous to my ears, but it's the truth. "Think about it."

She huffs, her eyes wide and incredulous. "We're not sure if you *are* Jesse's biological father. Let's take things one step at a time."

"Whatever you say. You call the shots," I agree easily even as determination to make Davie and Jesse mine solidifies in my belly.

I've never felt such an instant attraction to a woman.

Never felt so sure about anything in my life.

It's an uncomfortable sensation, but I'm not about to shrug it off. I'm forty-three-years-old. I've long given up on the idea of having a family of my own.

But Davie showed up on my ranch.

With news of my baby.

Even if the paternity test is negative, I'll still claim Jesse and his aunt. Partially because Cody sounds like an unreliable prick, but mostly because I'll do anything to protect this innocent woman and baby.

Davie needs help?

She can count on me.

# 7
## DAVIE

This man is more dangerous than I thought.

*Marry him?!*

Who would suggest such a thing to a stranger they just met?

Not a sane and responsible person.

But what worries me more than Cormac's proposal is my gut reaction to agree. Sure, I produced the expected outward incredulity, but inside, his plan makes a whole lot of sense.

*If he's Jesse's father.*

"Okay, well, first things first. We need to determine if you're Jesse's bio dad. Since it's court-mandated, you're required to use an approved lab for testing." I bite my lip, wishing Jessica had remembered—or known Cormac's last name at the ruling—because then the information would have been couriered to him, rather than me needing to track him down across state lines.

Cormac pulls out his phone and starts typing. "There's a doctor in town. Though it won't be official, maybe we can get a rapid test done before moving forward."

"Right... Wouldn't want to make the trip for nothing."

His head whips up so fast I jerk back in my seat, baffled over the fierceness in his gaze.

"I'm going to court with you no matter what," he says. "It's just a matter of knowing how strong our case will be. Married, so the bio aunt isn't a single mom, since the judge doesn't seem to approve of that, or married, so the bio aunt and bio dad are the obvious choice for placement."

"Wait, you'll marry me even if you're not Jesse's father?"

"Damn straight. Now, let's get going. Dr. Landish will meet us at the clinic for the test. We'll have to pick up Jesse to get his DNA, too."

Everything is moving so fast that I don't even protest when he guides me out the door with a large palm on my lower back.

We bypass my car for his truck before I remember Jesse's car seat. After switching directions, the two of us load into my sedan with Cormac behind the steering wheel, despite his too-large frame in the small space, and drive toward the B&B.

I text Linnea a brief update to prepare her for our arrival, but a few short sentences barely scratch the surface of how this morning is turning out.

Glancing at Cormac in my periphery, I try to sort out the picture he makes. Grizzled rancher with shaggy hair and glints of silver in his beard, suntanned and burly from working outside, and armed with an explosive temper. He's not exactly who I would have chosen as Jesse's dad.

Or a husband.

*You're not marrying the man. He's not serious about going through with a marriage.*

Surely, he can't be.

But the longer I stare, the more I sense Cormac's not the type of man to make idle promises.

# 8

## CORMAC

I've always been a decisive person.

*There's no place for wishy-washy while working the land.* That's what Dad used to say, and I carry those words with me every day.

When a man is only as good as his word, then he better be damn sure of each fucking decision.

Which is why I don't waste time second-guessing what's next: a rapid DNA test that ensures results in twenty-four hours.

Dr. Landish meets me on the sidewalk in front of her office while we wait for Davie to arrive with Jesse and her friend, Linnea. I dropped her off at the B&B three blocks away, so they should get here soon.

And I'll meet my potential son.

Shit, that sounds crazy even in my own head.

"A paternity test, huh?" Dr. Landish asks, curiosity coloring her tone. We don't know each other well, but she's handled a fair share of accidents on the ranch, so we're friendly enough.

"Yep. Surprises the hell out of me, too."

"If someone had asked me which of the Madsen brothers would require proof of fatherhood, my money would have been on Connor."

"Looks like you would have lost that bet, then." Though, I would've guessed the same.

Connor isn't exactly reckless, but he's less guarded than I am. Manages his time better since the majority of it is spent behind a computer.

He fucks for fun, while I fuck to forget the stresses of running a ranch.

Maybe that won't be a problem anymore.

Not if Davie and I end up getting married.

Sure, the work will still exist, but it'll mean more. It'll be for my family. To support them.

And knowing I have a beautiful wife and baby to come home to at the end of a long day? That's fucking priceless.

Davie's familiar sedan parks on the street, and I hurry to help her with the diaper bag she swings over her shoulder.

"I've got it," I say, carefully sliding the thick strap from her arm to mine and catching my first glimpse at Jesse, who's wide-eyed and babbling in his car seat.

"Oh... Um, thanks." Davie bends down to fiddle with the plastic car seat base, and immediately, my eyes fall to her ass, appreciating the round temptation before someone clears their throat.

Dragging my gaze away, I catch Davie's friend staring at me from over the car's roof. *Right.* This is my first time meeting my possible child, yet I'm busy ogling his curvy aunt.

"Let me hold him." I reach out for the baby carrier once it's free from its restraints, but Davie backs up.

"No, I've got him. You'll have plenty of time to carry him

around once we determine he's actually yours." A pink blush rises to Davie's cheeks. "Sorry. That sounded meaner than I meant it."

Her friend Linnea snickers as we gather on the sidewalk.

"No need to apologize, sweetheart." She doesn't trust me yet—not even to carry Jesse a few feet to the clinic—but that's okay. We have time, and I'm determined to win her over.

"Hi! You must be Davie, and this little cutie must be Jesse." Dr. Landish welcomes us into an empty waiting room then leads us to an exam room. "Cormac explained the situation, so I already have everything laid out. A couple of cheek swabs, then we'll be done."

"And we'll have results in twenty-four hours?"

"Yep."

Davie unbuckles Jesse from his carrier. "How accurate is the test?"

"Extremely accurate," Dr. Landish says as she dons a pair of gloves. "Like 99.9%. Court cases require a certain chain of custody, and there are some other trade-offs for speedy results, but accuracy isn't an issue."

I open my mouth for the swab while watching Davie with Jesse. His chubby fingers tug at her hair, while she lightly bounces him in her arms. The pang in my chest is sharp and immediate.

Jesse could be my son.

I study his tiny features, searching for clues. Are those my eyes? My Dad's ears? Is his dark hair from me or Davie's side of the family?

Only time, and this rapid DNA test, will tell.

———

I invite Davie, Linnea, and Jesse back to the ranch for lunch after we finish at the doctor's office. Fancy will have plenty of food to satisfy extra guests, and a casual meal together seems like a safe way to learn more about each other.

"Are you sure it's alright for us to drop in unannounced? I don't want to cause more work for someone," Davie says, worrying her plush bottom lip as we step inside the main house.

"It's fine. Fancy will be happy to have female company. Not to mention a baby. It's been a while since the ranch has had a kid on the property." Not since Deacon's son, Dylan, was a child.

The clatter of dishes and conversation greets us as we enter the large dining room. A long trestle table dominates the center of the room, meant to house every ranch employee and Madsen family member.

Slowly, the noise fades into confused silence. It's not often the Rocking M hosts women, let alone a baby.

"Who do we have here?" Fancy asks as she sets a platter of cornbread on the table.

Clearing my throat, suddenly feeling like a teenager bringing a girl home for the first time, I gesture toward our guests. "This is Davie, Linnea, and Jesse. They're here to..."

My words trail off. I don't want to announce my potential fatherhood to the entire ranch yet. I'm not ashamed, but it's not official. Not until Dr. Landish calls with the test results.

"Check out the ranch," Davie interjects, "and see if it's a good fit for my company. So far, so good." She forces a strained smile while her eyes beg me to support the lie.

"Right... Another corporate retreat might be coming."

Connor's brows twinge upward. "What company? I don't remember any emails or calls about an inquiry visit."

"We'll get into the details later. No shop talk at meal-times, right, Fancy?"

The older woman's eyes narrow, but she nods in agreement before ushering Davie and Linnea to empty chairs. I snag the seat next to Davie and start filling her plate with food.

"I can make my own plate," she whispers as the guys around the table begin chatting again.

"Of course, you can, but you don't have to. You've got Jesse in your lap." And it's the least I can do to take care of her.

Feeding Davie is one small way to prove I'm worth taking a chance on. She might have caught me at my worst this morning when I decked Garrett in the face, but I'm more than my temper.

I'm a man of my word. Honest and trustworthy. A provider.

I'd make a good husband to her and an excellent father for Jesse.

If she only gives me a chance.

# 9

## DAVIE

"Talk about a silver fox. Your sister sure knows how to pick them," Linnea says, fanning herself while I flip on my turn signal to merge onto the highway.

After Dr. Landish called yesterday to share the news—*yes, Cormac is Jesse's biological father*—it was decided that Cormac would follow us back home, so he could complete the official, court-approved testing.

Now, we're hours away from arriving at the tiny apartment Jesse and I used to share with his mom and having Cormac camped out on our couch.

Why did I invite him to stay with us? Despite spending a few hours together yesterday so Cormac and Jesse could bond, the man is still a stranger.

*A ruggedly handsome one, too.*

"This isn't new," I grouse. "Hot guys flock to Jessica."

The personalities of my sister's string of men may be sketchy and no-good, but their physical attractiveness has never been in question. Her type is always hot and full of bad habits, although Cormac seems to break the mold.

Owning and running a ranch is too dirty and back-breaking for her flaky ex-boyfriends. Plus, Cormac is older than her usual man.

"True… Even Cody is cute at first glance, then he opens his mouth." Linnea met Jessica's ex at the first custody hearing and grumbled about his fake concern for Jesse the entire way home afterwards.

"It's a shame when you think about it. Pretty privilege is a real thing," I say. "He could use it to his advantage, and instead, he wastes his life on drugs and causing trouble."

"At least you won't have to deal with him anymore. Cormac is lightyears better."

"Yeah, but he brings his own set of problems. I can't leave Jesse with a stranger just because they share blood. And I wouldn't feel right fighting him for custody when I'm the one who sought him out in the first place."

"You could always marry him," Linnea suggests, shrugging beneath her seatbelt.

"What?" My knuckles turn white around the steering wheel. I'd kept Cormac's proposal a secret because it was too ridiculous to consider, but now my best friend was suggesting the same thing? "What part of him being a stranger didn't you understand?"

"I'm serious." She starts ticking off points on her fingers. "The man owns a ranch, so you know he's responsible and stable—two of your top sought after traits in a partner. The judge favors fathers, and Cormac being married to Jesse's biological aunt solidifies you both as the best parents. Plus, it doesn't hurt that he's got that whole gruff cowboy thing going on."

*What the hell?* Linnea's reasons sounded eerily similar to Cormac's when he mentioned marriage at the Rocking M.

Minus the note about my dream man checklist.

Not that there's a real list, but Linnea isn't wrong about me craving security and stability in life. In a partner.

It's something I've been missing from the moment I realized my childhood wasn't like other kids'.

"We need to talk about your media consumption because I think all those fairytale books and movies are rotting your brain." Joking about potentially marrying Cormac stops me from privately admitting that maybe it's not such a wild idea, after all.

Like it might be the most reasonable thing for me to do.

Yeah, right, and the ten bucks in my wallet will magically transform into a one-hundred-dollar bill.

Unreasonable and *impossible*.

"We're talking about marriage. Vows of forever! Not whether or not I should get highlights," I say, silently urging my best friend to talk sense into me.

*Not* support Cormac's idea for keeping everyone together.

"It doesn't have to be forever. Just until everything is legal with Jesse. Sometimes the courts get things wrong, and I think gathering as much ammunition as possible to ensure you get Jesse, and not Cody, would be smart."

"Even if it means gaining a husband? A man whose first impression was punching an employee in the jaw?"

"You said that was justified," she points out.

"I said I could understand his reasoning, not that it was justified."

Linnea huffs. "Well, first impressions aren't always reliable. You've got to give him a chance, especially now that you know he's Jesse's dad. He seems determined to be good to both of you, judging by his actions in the past forty-eight hours."

She means how Cormac made sure I had plenty of food

and time to eat it during meals by preparing my plates and taking Jesse off my hands.

And how he carefully carted Jesse around his rustic farmhouse, softly describing the baby's family history.

It'd been sweet seeing the two of them together, and much too tempting to believe Cormac when he said he'd take care of us, no matter what.

No one has ever been able to fulfill that promise—not even my own parents who were biologically predisposed to love me—so trusting Cormac and marrying him?

I'm not ready to take that risk... *yet.*

# 10

## CORMAC

I have a son.

The entire trip from High Ridge to Medford, Oregon was spent processing the news. Not that almost nine hours of driving and thinking got me anywhere.

I'm pissed that Jessica waited to name me as Jesse's father until she got thrown in jail.

Frustrated that I've missed so much of my baby's early days, even if he'll never remember I wasn't there for him.

But beyond the anger and hurt, there's excitement, yearning, and definitely a sense of rightness—when it comes to both Overlands, Jesse *and* Davie.

During the frequent stops we made on the drive, I got to witness how sweet and protective Davie is of my son. She let me hold him briefly at a rest stop before swooping him back into her arms for a diaper change. Then, she allowed me to feed him a few hours later when we stopped for dinner.

It's obvious how much she loves Jesse and how wary she is of me.

I can't blame her, especially after what she witnessed at the ranch, but I'm determined to prove my worth. To replace that awful first impression with evidence that Davie can trust me.

Pale moonlight shimmers through the windshield, practically washed out by streetlights as we cruise through a suburban neighborhood, and I note the late hour on the dashboard. Thankfully, we're nearing the end of our journey and not still speeding down the highway.

Deer are a hazard almost everywhere these days, and the thought of Davie and Jesse crashing into a two-hundred-pound animal in her small sedan sends a spike of fear straight through my solar plexus.

An older apartment complex comes into view, and Davie parks in the cracked concrete lot. Swinging my truck around, I park next to her and get out.

She offered to let me stay on her couch for the night, since we have an appointment at the court-approved lab tomorrow morning. According to the internet, it'll be another one to two weeks before I'm officially confirmed as Jesse's biological dad.

But I can wait.

That will give me time to rearrange my life to fit a wife and kid.

And hopefully figure out how to convince Davie to marry me.

"Here we are." Davie sweeps her arm forward to encompass the tiny apartment, dumping her keys in a ceramic bowl.

Linnea took off a few minutes ago after being repeatedly assured that we'd be fine alone. It's the first time we haven't had a buffer since our first meeting.

"It's nice," I say. "Cozy."

Photos decorate the walls. Nature shots and family pictures. First, with Davie and a woman who must be Jessica, then more with Jesse added to the mix.

"You don't have to be polite. I know it's not what you're used to at the ranch, but we get by alright."

"It keeps you and Jesse safe and warm. That makes it good in my books." Leaning closer to a framed photograph resting on a side table, I point to the woman smiling beside Davie. "Is this Jessica?"

"You don't recognize her?"

Shame burns the tips of my ears. "I sound like an asshole, but no, not really." If I really tried, maybe she'd become more familiar, but I doubt it.

The anniversary of my dad's death is the one time I give myself permission to cut loose. Grieving and drinking. Those two things are all I have the capacity for, though clearly, I worked up enough energy to father a child this last time.

"Maybe it's for the best." She sighs and carries a sleeping Jesse to her room. "Sometimes I barely recognize my sister, and I practically raised her."

"You did?"

"Please don't count that against me. I love Jesse and would never—"

"Whoa..." My hands land on her shoulders to stop the spiraling. "No one is using anything against you. I was just curious. You can't be blamed for your sister's actions."

Davie droops beneath my palms, and instinctively, my thumbs dig into her stiff muscles, praying a massage might soothe her nerves.

"A judge might blame me," she whispers. There's a brittleness to her voice, like she's worried about this for longer than just tonight. Like one careful strike of a judge's gavel may cause an irreparable crack in her life.

"That's not going to happen." Unable to resist anymore, I tug her into my arms for a hug.

Jesse lays sleeping in the crib where she placed him earlier, and as I stare at my son over Davie's shoulder, my hold on his aunt tenses.

No one will separate Jesse and Davie, least of all me.

I've claimed them as my own, and that's all anyone needs to know if they decide to fuck with them.

Because I will fight to protect them—*always*—with everything I am.

# 11

CORMAC: Made it home safe.

DAVIE: *Thumbs up emoji*

CORMAC: ...

CORMAC: There's something that's been on my mind, but I don't want you to take it the wrong way.

DAVIE: Okay...

CORMAC: You said you 'practically raised' your sister. Why? Where were your parents?

DAVIE: That's a fair question. Our dad abandoned us when we were young. Our mom kind of checked out after he left, until she started dating again. The man in her life was always more important than her kids. Honestly, Jessica inherited some of that, though she tried to be better for Jesse at first.

CORMAC: I'm sorry they failed you. Thanks for telling me.

DAVIE: Well, if we're gonna have awkward conversations... LOL Might as well do it over text.

DAVIE: I'm not judging, but why don't you remember Jessica? She usually makes a splash wherever she goes.

CORMAC: The answer doesn't reflect well on me.

DAVIE: Does that mean you're not going to tell me?

CORMAC: No, I'm just warning you while working out how to explain, although it's not really complicated.

CORMAC: My dad died three years ago. The ranch wasn't doing well because he refused to listen to Connor or myself when it came to new ideas. When he passed, we inherited the ranch 50/50 with all its problems, and part of me is still angry at Dad for being so stubborn and saddling us with such a mess. Then I feel guilty for feeling mad.

DAVIE: Understandable. Those are valid feelings.

CORMAC: Thanks, sweetheart.

CORMAC: Anyway, it's an emotional few days of grief, anger, and shame, and it's fueled by alcohol. *This is the not so pretty part: I wallow and drink. Get drunk off my ass. I'm guessing it was then when your sister approached me, or maybe I approached her, I don't know. But that's why I don't remember her or anything about that night.

DAVIE: It's hard for me to imagine you that way. I know we don't know each other well, but I've met Jessica's ex-boyfriends who loved getting drunk. Our mom had a few thrown in there, too, so you learn to recognize the type. Just from our brief interactions, you don't really seem like the kind of guy who enjoys getting blackout drunk.

CORMAC: I wouldn't say I enjoy it… But it does the job of dulling the pain of Dad's absence and what that dredges up. The anniversary of his death is the one free pass I give myself. Otherwise, you're right, and I don't lose control like that.

DAVIE: Good to know.

CORMAC: Do you regret coming to find me now?

DAVIE: No. You're Jesse's dad, and you deserve to know each other. Besides, I'm not sure what's worse: you not remembering a one-night stand with my sister, or recalling the night and pining after Jessica.

CORMAC: Definitely no pining happening here.

CORMAC: At least, not for her…

———

DAVIE: *Picture of Jesse laughing* Thought you might want another snapshot of him!

CORMAC: Always!

CORMAC: *Shares picture of baby room with Connor, Deacon, and Briggs smiling in the background* His room is almost done. I can't wait for the two of you to get here.

DAVIE: I can't believe we're actually moving to High Ridge.

CORMAC: You're not thinking about changing your mind, are you?

DAVIE: Depends on what my room looks like... JK! Everything is moving fast, but it's fine. We're fine.

CORMAC: I can practically hear your anxious thoughts from here. Do we need to have another phone call where I remind you of all the reasons this will be good for you and Jesse?

DAVIE: *Nooo GIF* I'm on board. Trust me. I just wish we were past the transitional stage and settled. I'll feel better once life gets back to normal.

CORMAC: Don't worry, we'll get there. Until then, I'm here for whatever you need.

DAVIE: Thanks, I appreciate that.

DAVIE: Who's that guy with your brother and Deacon? He's the one from the hardware store who told me where to find you.

CORMAC: Yeah, he mentioned that you two might have met. That's Briggs, another one of my good friends. We've known each other since high school.

DAVIE: Oh, wow! What are the chances he'd be the one to lead me to you?

CORMAC: Small towns, baby. Small fucking towns.

# 12

## DAVIE

"The court sent your paternity test results, Mr. Madsen. It appears that you are Jesse Overland's biological father. Congratulations," my lawyer says through the speakerphone. The three of us are conferenced together on one line, since Cormac had to return to Washington after having his cheek swab at the lab.

While I haven't seen him in person the past few weeks, he's made sure to video call and text each day to check on me and Jesse.

The topic of marriage hasn't come up again, but now that we know he's officially Jesse's dad, it's the next logical step, especially since he asked Jesse and me to move in with him.

What a rollercoaster of events my life has turned into lately.

Find Jesse's bio dad? Check.

Ensure Jesse's custody by moving in and marrying Cormac? TBD.

Part of me thinks the plan is ridiculous. Why not just move in with the man until I trust Jesse in his care? Then I can find a cheap apartment in High Ridge to remain close. Do we really need to exchange vows?

But then I imagine the judge frowning upon the two of us 'shacking up' versus committing to something permanent—even if it is just a piece of paper tying us together.

Besides, if I'd learned I had a secret kid, I wouldn't want to be separated for longer than necessary. Cormac has been incredibly patient and calm. I can't imagine most men would handle the news of a one-night stand resulting in a baby as well as he has.

Of course, he could be bitching to his family and friends about *those Overland sisters* trapping him with an unwanted child, but somehow, I don't think that's the case.

Our short phone conversations have been devoid of bitterness and angst. Tension and awkwardness have been the norm, and those have come from me.

Frankly, I prefer our texting conversations. It's easier for me to talk to him virtually.

"A court date has been set for a month from now. That's when the judge will rule on custody. Until then, Jesse will remain in his aunt's care."

Cormac grunts in understanding before the lawyer lays out our next steps and ends his side of the call.

When it's just the two of us, a weighted silence hangs over the line. There's a lot to digest between learning Jesse's true parentage and waiting another four weeks to finalize custody.

"Have you given any more thought to the idea of marriage?"

Despite knowing the question was coming, it's still a shock to hear. My breathing picks up as a flush of heat dampens my forehead and underarms in nervous sweat.

Cormac doesn't wait for me to answer. He plows on

with his pitch, while I focus on not hyperventilating or spiraling into a panic attack.

"I don't mean to rush you, and we have some time, but with you and Jesse coming to live with me on the ranch. It seems like the best next step," he says.

Picking at a thread on my shirt, I swallow my nerves and say the first thing that pops into my head that's *not* about marrying Cormac. "Did I tell you my boss approved a move across state lines? I've always worked from home but the taxes work differently, I guess. Anyway, that's sorted, so it's just a matter of packing."

"You mentioned your boss on our last call. Remember I'm taking care of the move. A team is hired to pack and haul everything here."

"You really don't have to—"

"I want to, Davie, so don't worry about it. Consider it done."

My shoulders sag as I stare at the furniture and shelves of books and various knickknacks surrounding me, and that's just the living room. My bedroom, kitchen, and Jessica's bedroom with Jesse's things is full of stuff, too.

"Okay... thanks," I murmur, relaxing into the couch while my gaze fixates on a crack in the ceiling. This apartment really wasn't big enough for two adults and a baby, but aside from the size issue, it's not in the best shape either.

A fact I ignored because the rent was cheap.

Residing on a massive ranch like Cormac's will be a totally new experience.

"When the movers send their final instructions for the day, let me know. I'm notifying my landlord about breaking the lease later today."

I'm not looking forward to the huge chunk of money

that will cost, but it's not like I can ask Cormac to move here. There's not enough room, and he can't leave the Rocking M.

And I'm definitely not asking him for help paying the lease-breaking fee. He's already doing too much.

"Sounds like a plan," he pauses, and a horse whinnies in the background. "Davie?"

"Yeah?"

"Thank you for trusting me. I know you didn't ask to be thrown into the middle of all this, but I'm grateful my son has someone like you. Everything is going to be fine. You're not alone, and you won't be anymore. I promise you that."

I swallow hard at his kind words. Praise is a rarity in my life, which makes each drop of appreciation as precious as gold.

Tears fill my eyes at his continual kindness. How in the world did my sister get lucky enough to have this man even for one night? How did she manage to get pregnant by *him* rather than the dozens of douchebags in her past?

A gnawing sensation that feels suspiciously like jealousy sprouts in my belly.

Jealous of my younger sister? The one currently in jail for the next two years?

Me, the responsible eldest daughter, jealous over the man she had for one night?

*Not smart, Davie. Not fucking smart.*

# 13
## CORMAC

The county courthouse and town hall sit next to each other on a block of green and brown grass in the middle of High Ridge—separate from the rest of the buildings along Main Street.

"Looks like our new mayor is trying to make good on those promises to revive the town—starting with her domain," Connor muses as we watch a team of landscapers work to prepare the messy flowerbeds and patchy grass for spring's arrival.

"I'm glad. Miller let things go to shit." Jeb Miller's father had been an honorable man and helped High Ridge prosper during his tenure; his son hadn't inherited the same temperament or wisdom.

Which was why when Brenda Castillo decided to run against the usually unopposed Miller family, she won.

Tugging on my cuffed sleeve, my eyes drift away from a guy clearing dead leaves behind some bushes to the parking lot.

Davie should be here soon with Jesse and Linnea, who will serve as one of our witnesses.

"Nervous?" Connor asks. When I told him about Jesse and my plans to marry Davie, he'd offered very little resistance. He knew how much I wanted a family. Knew I'd never abandon my own kid.

If he held any doubts about marrying a stranger, my brother kept them to himself—choosing to support me without judgment.

My best friends, Deacon and Briggs, were another story. Deacon had voiced his concern several times while we worked together on the ranch, and Briggs's attitude stemmed from how he first met Davie that fateful day at the hardware store.

The fact that she sought me out to deliver the news of my son made him question her intentions. As if she intended to trap me into marriage all along, despite it being me persuading her to say yes.

I spot a grey sedan in the parking lot and release the pent-up breath in my lungs. "Not anymore. They're here."

My long strides eat up the space between us, barely giving me enough time to drink in the sight of Davie in a light blue sundress before I pull her into my arms.

"You came."

A surprised laugh puffs against my neck. "Of course, I did. You think I'd bail? Our things are already at your ranch."

"Our ranch," I correct, reluctantly letting her go, and reaching inside the car for Jesse. My boy looks adorable in his little tuxedo tee. "Hey, kiddo. Ready to be Daddy's best man?"

"I thought that was my job," Connor says from the sidewalk.

"Face it. You can't beat those chubby cheeks." Linnea

pats my brother's arm in commiseration. Clearly, she's lost out on Davie's list of priorities, thanks to my boy, too.

Connor places a dramatic hand over his heart. "I've been replaced. Thirty-some-odd years as my brother's favorite gone, just like that." He snaps his fingers.

Rolling my eyes, I heft Jesse higher on my chest, forgoing his carrier for the trip inside. "Who said you were my favorite?" I tease, sparing a glance at my watch. "We should go. Our appointment with the judge is in fifteen minutes. We don't want to be late for our own wedding."

For a Monday morning, the halls are busier than I expected. The sound of heels striking marble floors echoes in the lobby as we study a directory before heading to the second floor.

A clerk greets us with a professional smile, asking us to sign a few papers, then we're instructed down the hall to wait for the judge to call on us.

When a bailiff ushers our group forward, the hush of an empty courtroom accentuates the weight of what Davie and I are about to do.

We're getting married.

We'll legally be tied together until death do us part.

"Good morning," the judge says, "IDs, please."

The four of us place our licenses on the raised platform. While he signs more papers and checks the IDs, I hand Jesse over to Connor while Linnea pulls out her phone. I'm not sure if she's taking pictures or videoing the ceremony, but either way, I'm thankful for her foresight.

"Okay, face each other, and we'll conduct the vows."

Unlike previous weddings I've attended, these vows are professional rather than romantic, especially when prompted by the no-nonsense tone of the judge.

Seeds of regret niggle into my mind. Maybe we should

have waited. Davie deserves flowers and music. She deserves more than a perfunctory recitation of a basic oath.

"If you'd like, you may kiss the bride." For the first time since we entered the room, a glimmer of happiness shone on the judge's wrinkled features.

Davie's eyes widen and the slightest shiver runs down her body as I draw her closer with a hand on her waist.

Cupping her cheek, I bend my head then pause, searching for permission. I won't force Davie to do something she doesn't want to, no matter how much I crave the feel of her lips beneath mine.

She's my wife now; we have time.

But hell, if that doesn't stop me from praying for—*that*. Davie's lashes flutter closed as her head tips back in silent consent, and I don't waste a second.

Our mouths connect in a gentle brush before I dare to swipe my tongue over her lower lip. There's the slightest sigh, letting me inside the sweet cavern of her mouth, and it's then that I know I'm done for.

This is my last first kiss, and it belongs to my wife, Davie Madsen.

# 14
## DAVIE

Sunrise on the ranch whispers of warmth and safety. As orange, yellow, and pink stretch across the Washington sky, a sense of calm wraps around me even as I snuggle deeper into my long cardigan.

I shouldn't feel so comfortable.

Not with a baby to raise and an older rancher who is now my husband.

The screen door creaks before heavy footsteps vibrate through the porch's floorboards with Cormac's arrival. Strong arms bracket my sides against the porch railing, and a wave of heat sweeps down my backside from the intimate brush of lips on the side of my neck.

"Morning, wife." Four little letters spoken in that rough, gravelly tone shouldn't have such an effect on me, but the immediate shiver that runs over my skin before settling between my thighs in a dull ache isn't easy to ignore.

*God, we've been married for less than twenty-four hours. How am I supposed to survive months of this?*

We haven't discussed divorce, but surely, once everything is settled with Jesse and our marriage is no longer necessary, he'll want to end it, right?

"Good morning," I say quietly, partially in deference to the early hour, but mostly due to the growing confusion at my feelings for this man.

Cormac had a one-night stand with my younger sister and fathered a child with her. Full stop. Any wayward attraction threatening to bloom should shrivel into a dead carcass each time I remember that fact.

Even if he is my husband.

*It's a legal arrangement to protect my nephew.*

*Nothing more.*

So why am I leaning into his firm strength as if this is a cozy morning with the man I love and not a man who is totally off-limits?

"Where's your coat? It's freezing out here." He curls the edges of his thick Carhartt jacket around my sides, though there's absolutely no hope of it meeting in the middle between Cormac's bulk and my fluffiness.

I appreciate the gesture, though.

Too much.

"I like the cold. It helps me think."

"Don't think too hard," he gently reprimands. "It's too early to start worrying about the future again. We've done all we can to secure custody of Jesse. He's my son. The court can't deny it."

"That's not what—" I cut myself off.

*If only Jesse was my main concern.*

But no, I'm more focused on his dad. *My husband.* The man whose kiss still lingers on my lips, despite it happening yesterday. It doesn't help that Linnea sent a photo of the moment with capital *H.O.T.* "Never mind...

You're right. It's too early to stress about things out of my control."

Cormac hums in his throat and carefully turns me in his arms until I'm facing him. "You're thinking about us."

A hot blush rises to my cheeks. There shouldn't be an *us*. There was a *Cormac and Jessica*, and that should have been enough to crush these wayward feelings.

"How about a distraction from the spiraling, hmm?" A rough fingertip drags down my cheek and throat until his callused palm encircles the vulnerable column. "I've always dreamed of waking up and kissing my wife good morning before chores. What do you say we start the tradition today?"

I gulp at the heat in his eyes, secretly reveling in the danger of his hand around my neck. My fingers tangle around his belt loops as I sway closer.

"Is that smart?" I whisper.

"Baby, it's fucking necessary."

We both lean forward until our lips meet in the middle of the chilly air, unable to resist temptation any longer. The fog of our mingled breaths wafts over my cheeks as Cormac's tongue tangles with mine, and I give myself twenty seconds of blissful freedom.

Freedom to enjoy kissing my husband.

Freedom from thoughts about Jessica.

But then reality sets in like an icy pick to the heart, and I break the hold Cormac has on me—running inside the house and away from my taboo feelings.

# 15

## CORMAC

Davie shuffles into the kitchen like everything is normal, rinsing out her empty coffee mug then placing it in the dishwasher beside the sink.

She keeps her eyes low and focused on each task. Each movement reveals a slight tremble in her hands as if the pressure of maintaining a calm veneer needs that small release, or else she'll lose control.

"Are you thirsty? You've been up for hours, right? I can pour you another coffee or—"

"Davie." She flinches at the sound of her name, and that's the last straw. Rounding the kitchen island, I herd my nervous wife backward until she bumps into the marble countertop.

My hands sink into her hips before lifting her onto the counter. The cotton sleep shirt and cardigan bunch under her ass, exposing thick, pale thighs that naturally fall open to accommodate my wide girth.

"What... We shouldn't..."

My finger lands on her parted lips. "Shh... It's my turn to talk now." I let the digit pull on the soft flesh, the wet, pink gleam inside her mouth stirring all sorts of fantasies of other wet, pink parts of her. "You're scared, I know. That's why I've let you dictate our pace, but we're married now, and I think it's time I've made myself clear."

"C-Clear?" Davie gulps, and I gently trace the subtle action. Down her vulnerable throat. Over the strain of a peaked nipple through her shirt. Past her round belly.

Until my palm rests on her trembling thigh, my thumb dipping into the crease where smooth skin meets cotton panties.

Cotton shirt. Cotton panties. Practical.

Just like my girl.

"Jesse isn't the only one I want out of this arrangement," I admit, stroking the mound of her pussy through thin material until dry gives way to damp, and the change has me ignoring the slow tease in favor of sliding my eager fingers inside her panties to feel the intoxicating wetness for myself.

Davie's hands wrap around the edge of the counter like I wish they'd wrap around me, her knuckles turning white with the pressure.

A shudder wracks her body as she offers the tiniest bit of consent—rocking her pelvis forward so the tips of my fingers are engulfed in her clenching heat.

"The moment I saw you on my ranch, I wanted you, even if I figured it'd be impossible for such a sweet creature to let me near after what you witnessed."

"You…" Davie's eyes fluttered shut then opened again as she licked her lips, struggling to find her words. "You should learn how to control your temper."

Chuckling, I shake my head. "Oh, sweetheart… When it comes to someone hurting what's mine, defending them will win out every time." Like with my son and his aunt.

They're mine, now, and if someone dares to fuck that up, they'll learn how well I control my temper.

So well that they end up six feet deep somewhere in the back forty.

"I'm not yours." Davie whimpers after a brutal thrust of my fingers in retribution for voicing such a lie. "At least not like that. We're married on paper for Jesse's sake. I can't sleep with you. It wouldn't be responsible."

"And you're always responsible, aren't you?"

"I have to be. It's my job."

"Actually, it's not. Your job is to care for Jesse, and we both know you're phenomenal at it." My boy couldn't do better than my sweet little wife. "Otherwise? You're free to do what you want. Break free, baby."

My free hand lifts to cup her pinkened cheek. "Here with me? You don't have to worry about a damn thing. I'm your shield, and you've seen how fiercely I protect what's mine."

# 16

## DAVIE

Cormac becomes a blur through the tears threatening to fall. He's saying all the right things, but he's the wrong man.

I can't sleep with my sister's baby daddy.

It doesn't matter that he's my husband.

He's Jessica's ex-one-night stand.

"Tell me what's going on in that head of yours. I know you're overthinking when all you should be doing is feeling."

His thumb swipes over my clit to remind me of the delicious rhythm of his hand between my thighs.

As if I could forget.

How I'm managing a coherent conversation at a time like this is a damn miracle.

"This isn't right," I say. "You're my nephew's father. You're my sister's—"

"I'm your husband," he grits out. "I don't remember your sister, but I sure as hell will remember you. There's no fucking comparison."

"It doesn't feel that way. It feels wrong. Like I'm stepping into my sister's place. Like I'm her replacement, and we're nothing alike. If you wanted Jessica, then I don't understand how you can want me."

There. My worst fear announced. Being his second choice, even if logically I understand it was just sex between them.

Cormac removes his fingers from my pussy and holds them in the air in front of my face. "See this? See how wet you are for me?" His other hand frees my grip on the counter and places my palm over the large bulge running down his thigh. "Feel that? Feel how hard I am for you?"

"This has nothing to do with your fucking sister. This is about you and me. You're not a consolation prize for Jessica. I doubt I could pick her out of a lineup; she's that fuzzy in my memory. But you?"

He huffs like an angry grizzly and clamps my chin between his thumb and forefinger. "I'd find you from the merest whisper of your breath. The faintest hint of your scent. Because you're engraved on my bones."

His lips stamp a harsh kiss to mine before trailing over my cheek to my ear as he resumes teasing my clit. "Davie Madsen." Sharp teeth nip at my earlobe before a hot tongue licks away the sting. "My wife... The people in your life failed you, but I won't."

"You can't promise that."

"Yes, I can. Because no matter what happens, what mistakes I make, I'll fight like hell to fix them."

The line between right and wrong blurs with each kiss and caress. Pleasure blooms and pops, and I can't resist grabbing onto Cormac, desperate for release. For stability. For reassurance.

"Cormac..." I moan, my lungs fighting for air.

"Say it again," he commands. "Say my name."

"Cormac... Cormac... Cor—" The crash of the orgasm tears a strangled scream from my throat.

Jesse's down the hall sleeping. *I can't wake him.*

Cormac's strong arm around my back anchors me in place as he lightens his touch at my core, carefully easing me through my climax until I'm a sweaty mess collapsed on his chest.

His bearded cheek nuzzles into the hollow between my neck and shoulder, and I shiver at his tender kiss—a brand of ownership in my pleasure-addled mind.

"We're spending the day together. You, me, and Jesse. Like a family," Cormac growls. "I'll be back to pick you up at noon."

And with one last kiss, he's gone, leaving me wondering what the hell I'm doing.

# 17
## CORMAC

Amusement twitches along Davie's cheeks while I attempt to strap into Jesse's chest carrier. The navy backpack is supposed to be easy to wear, and to be fair, the buckle system is simple enough. The problem is the size, or rather, *my* size.

"We might need a strap extender," I grouch, loosening the woven strap to its limit to fit around my waist.

Davie chuckles, tickling Jesse's tummy to get him to laugh, too. "If it fits me, it'll fit you."

I grunt in doubt, but eventually, all the straps are clicked into place, and I'm ready to take Jesse off her hands.

After this morning's events, I've been looking forward to sharing this time with Jesse and Davie—a peaceful walking tour of the ranch.

Deacon and a few of the guys are covering my chores this afternoon, which means I'm free to show my family their new home.

Especially since there hasn't been a lot of opportunity for Davie to explore yet.

"This kid's growing like a weed," I say once Jesse is

settled facing forward. "It's amazing how much he's changed in so little time. He was practically a different baby when we first met."

"I know. I thought the same thing after he was born, too." Davie's steps falter as we head outside to the barn. "Sorry, I probably shouldn't mention those first few months."

There's a tightening in my chest from the knowledge that I'll never get those early, newborn days back. Davie sent me pictures through texts, but none of them came with the sound of my baby's cry or that newborn smell.

"No, you should. I want to hear everything about him, especially the things I missed." The barn's large sliding door is open, so we walk inside to the scent of hay, animals, and manure, heading toward my horse, Rollo, for introductions.

Davie shares how she and Jessica adapted to a newborn—Davie doing the lion's share of feedings and changings because her sister would go off with Cody doing god knows what.

"Of course, at the time, I didn't know she was still seeing him. She told me they were done. For good." Her fingers gently pet Rollo's forehead. "I chose to believe her because a part of me dreams of the day Jessica changes her life around."

"Maybe prison will do that for her." I have no sympathy for the mother of my child. Davie tries not to speak negatively about her sister, but facts are facts, and I can read between the lines.

Jessica is a selfish and immature woman.

She probably shouldn't be a mother, but I can't regret her decision to have Jesse anyway.

"Maybe... So, you have horses and cattle. What other animals live here?"

The shift in topic lightens the mood as I gesture for Davie to follow me back outside. She wants to forget about her sister's drama?

I'll show her every cute and fluffy critter the Rocking M has to offer.

# 18

## DAVIE

My pacing wears on the carpet in the guest room Cormac gave me. I could tell he was reluctant to give me a separate space, but I appreciate he didn't force me to move into his bedroom immediately upon our marriage.

Though sleeping alone on my wedding night wasn't exactly how I always imagined it.

"And I could change that tonight," I say aloud, "if I can stop being a coward."

After a tour around the Rocking M today, we spent dinner together with Connor, Fancy, and some of the other ranch employees. Everyone congratulated us again on our nuptials, then moved on to casual conversation—a relief since I don't like being the center of attention.

"Ugh," I groan. I check the baby monitor in my hand and see that Jesse is still knocked out in his crib in the nursery Cormac created.

A sleeping baby means I have free time.

And what do I want to do with it? Jump my newfound husband.

I mean, it's really not fair that I'm married to a sexy silver fox who clearly knows his way around a woman's body.

And I'm still a virgin bride. There should be some kind of law against that.

Even if it's my own damn fault, because I let this thing with Jessica get in my head.

*Forget about your sister, Cormac has. This is your life. Take the reins.*

The pep talk gets me out of my bedroom and into Cormac's after knocking on his door to no answer. The sound of the shower comes from his ensuite bathroom, and I wonder if it'd be better if I come back later.

*No, Davie. Do this now before you chicken out.*

My legs carry me forward to the threshold of the bathroom. Steam billows above the open shower stall. It's one of those fancy layouts where there's no lip. The tile just runs in a slight slope into the shower section where it drains, and a glass wall separates the space from the freestanding tub.

Cormac sees me immediately based on the sudden tension in his body.

His wet, *naked* body.

A cascade of water spills over his sun-darkened skin and firm muscles all the way down to the heavy cock resting in his fist.

*Holy fuck, did I just walk in on him jerking off?*

"Davie, is everything alright?" he asks like everything is normal, and he's not standing in front of me naked, his huge palm lightly stroking a rather large erection.

A knot forms in my throat. "Everything's fine." I wave the baby monitor in the air. "Jesse's asleep."

"Good," he says. "Did you need something?"

Curiosity and hunger mingle in his gaze.

It's the latter that gives me the confidence to step closer. "I..." Panic sets in as words desert me.

*I want you to fuck me?*

*Take my virginity?*

*Put me out of my misery?*

All of these questions are a possibility in my scrambled, too-nervous brains.

"What do you need, sweetheart?"

"We're married," I say stupidly. As if he wasn't at the courthouse, too.

"We are."

"But we're not really married yet," I add.

One of his brows tip upward. "We're not?"

"Well, you know..." I gesture vaguely. "If this were medieval times, marriage isn't legitimate until it's consummated, right? So, I mean, technically, that hasn't happened yet."

"I don't think the judge is going to check if we've consummated our marriage," he teases, thankfully interrupting my ramble.

"No, no, of course not. It's just that—"

"Davie," he mercifully cuts in.

"Yes?"

"Take off your clothes, and get in here."

"Oh, okay." My shoulders slump with relief at having something to do as I place the baby monitor on the counter.

My clothes fall in a disheveled pile on the floor.

My arms cross over my chest as I scamper into the heated shower.

"So..." I drawl, unsure again.

"Come here. Closer," Cormac commands.

He releases his cock from his grip, and my eyes can't

help but widen at the sight of his thickness up close and personal.

Geez, do I really want all of that inside me? *Fuck yeah*.

Once I'm within reach, Cormac guides me towards the tile wall until my breasts and belly button touch the cool marble.

"Since you're so nervous, maybe this will help you relax: facing away from me." His palms smooth over my skin, whatever soap he was using easing the glide of rough over soft.

He slides his fingers between me and the wall to cup my breasts, pinching my nipples, and my back bows as I gasp at the immediate difference between cool tile and warm skin.

"That's it," he murmurs. "There's no need to be nervous. I'm your husband, and you, *my wife*, need me. Need my cock, don't you?" He tugs on the bottom of my ear with his teeth before kissing the delicate skin below.

I whimper and nod, and that's all he needs before continuing his exploration.

One hand remains on my breast. The other dips between my thighs. Spreads my arousal from slit to clit.

"So wet for me, baby. You're already primed to take this thick cock, aren't you?"

"Yes," I breathe, "please, don't make me wait." I've waited years to know a man's skin on mine. His heavy girth filling me to the brim.

I don't want to wait any longer.

"Never... What my wife wants, she gets. Always," he growls. His teasing ends with the mushroom head of his cock bumping at my opening and slowly pushing forward.

I arch onto my toes, never having experienced this kind of pleasurable burn before in my life. It doesn't hurt.

There's just a feeling of fullness, of being stretched to my limits.

When Cormac bottoms out, he groans, then sets a leisurely pace, grinding his hips against my ass as I'm sandwiched between him and the wall.

Everything is steamy, hazy, a dream.

Our breath, the water. Pants and groans of pleasure. It's more than I ever imagined.

And I'm experiencing it with my husband, my sister's one-night stand.

Somehow, that fact doesn't matter when Cormac hits a particularly sensitive spot, and I come with a cry of surprise, his own release not far behind.

As I wilt in his arms from the force of my climax, Jessica and all the reasons why I shouldn't fall for my husband evaporate.

I'm too cozy—too safe and satisfied in Cormac's arms —to worry about the future right now.

# 19
## DAVIE

"Jesse and Davie Madsen?" a nurse calls into the waiting room, and I give a little wave before grabbing Jesse and following her to an exam room.

The use of Cormac's last name for both of us surprises me. Despite our marriage, I haven't officially switched from Overland to Madsen. Too many questions hang in the air for me to go through the trouble of paperwork for a legal change that might not be permanent.

Sure, Cormac and I are in a good place.

A really good place if I remember the way his bearded cheeks felt between my thighs this morning as he woke me up with his tongue.

But good things never last.

Not in my experience, at least.

There's a knock on the door, then Dr. Landish walks in with a smile. "Hello, again!" She sits on a rolling stool and scans the computer monitor with our charts. "Looks like today we're establishing care, is that right?"

"Yep." Cormac insisted I get set up with a local GP, too, when I mentioned scheduling Jesse for an appointment.

Growing up, our family relied on publicly funded healthcare, and even then, doctor's visits were infrequent. It wasn't until I landed a job offering health insurance that I finally saw someone regularly.

So, Cormac's concern for my wellbeing is... *different*.

And way too intoxicating.

Everything about my husband—his gentleness with Jesse, the way he looks after us, the mind-blowing sex—weakens the barricades around my heart.

Decades of protecting myself, of being responsible for not only myself but Jessica, and at times, our mother, dashed to dust because of one rough rancher with a heart of gold.

Dr. Landish adjusts her stethoscope to listen to Jesse's heart and lungs. "Sounds good. Where's Daddy today?"

"Dealing with an emergency. He wanted to come, but I told him he can attend the next one."

"I'm surprised he agreed. Cormac is a good guy, and he seems intent on doing everything possible to be a great dad. He actually called me to ask about what all I'd be doing during this visit."

A puff of laughter bursts free. "Seriously? Yet he still fought me about staying back at the ranch." Ugh, the man is impossibly sweet. "Deacon came by right before we left. I'm not sure what happened, but he was adamant that Cormac had to be there."

"Those three." Dr. Landish shakes her head.

"Three?"

"Cormac, Deacon, and Briggs. I haven't actually met Briggs, but I've heard the stories about him. I'm not originally from High Ridge, only moved here a few months ago, but my patients love to gossip about that trio. Especially now that news has spread about Jesse's parentage."

My brows wing upward. I haven't officially met Briggs either—outside our brief run-in at the hardware store when I had no clue who he was—but Cormac hasn't shared anything gossip-worthy about the man.

Jesse, and by extension, me, on the other hand...

"Guess that means they're probably talking about our quickie marriage, too, huh?" I ask.

Dr. Landish winces. "Yeah... Everyone is curious. I mean, Cormac is a catch. A handsome silver fox who runs a successful ranch? Lots of women were disappointed when they heard about you."

"Oh, god." My face drops into my hands as I groan.

"Sorry to be the bearer of bad news," she jokes, patting my arm. "If you ever want to commiserate over drinks about small towns and the gossip mill, I'm still on the search for local friends."

"Can a doctor be friends with a patient?" I'm not opposed to hanging out with Dr. Landish. Honestly, I could use a friend, too, since Linnea is hours away in Oregon.

"It's a bit of a grey area," she admits. "But this is a small town, and things work differently here. If everyone avoided relationships based on a conflict of interest, then no one would be able to connect."

"True... Though I should probably call you something other than Dr. Landish outside the office."

"Ah, good point. Call me Autumn." She playfully offers her hand in greeting, and I accept with a grin. "Nice to meet you."

"Now, let's get you checked out before your husband calls the office wondering what's taking us so long. I wouldn't put it past him to drive out here to make sure you're both okay."

"Me neither," I say, shocked by the confidence I feel.

Cormac would worry about us if the appointment dragged on. He'd worry because he'd be thinking about us. We wouldn't be forgotten just because there's something more important in his life.

And somewhere in the vicinity of my heart, another brick wall crumbles to ashes.

# 20

## CORMAC

"I can't believe we both have sons." Deacon shakes his head in disbelief before taking a sip of his beer.

"Better late than never," I joke. Deacon had his son, Dylan, at sixteen with his then-girlfriend. Now, Dylan is old enough to be my own son's father when our kids should have grown up together.

"Congratulations, brother," Connor cheers, "you finally have everything you wanted—a beautiful wife and a cute as fuck kid."

Briggs snorts, refusing to clink his beer bottle with the rest of ours at the center of the table. "Yeah, I mean, it really could have been any woman and kid, though. You just wanted a family. Handy that this one popped onto your doorstep."

"Jesus!"

"Not cool, asshole."

"What's the matter with you?" I place a protective hand over Jesse's chest, where he rests on my thigh. "I know you disagree with the speed of things between us, but I've had enough of your bitching. Disrespect my wife again, and that will be the last time. Understand?"

Briggs grunts and dips his chin in acknowledgment, though he doesn't apologize for his harsh words.

Words that stick with me through the rest of the evening, on the drive home, and lying in bed waiting for Davie to finish her nightly routine.

Was Briggs right?

Would I have immediately married any woman who popped up on my ranch?

Am I using Davie to fulfill my dreams while ignoring what she needs? Sure, she needs me to retain custody of Jesse, but is that enough to justify everything else I've asked of her?

My gut rejects the possibility, but my head... It replays Briggs's words over and over again.

"What's wrong?" Davie asks, sliding beneath the covers next to me.

"I've always wanted a family. It's never been a secret," I admit, staring at the ceiling, afraid to see her reaction to this next part. "You and Jesse are a dream come true for me, but do you feel used? Like I was so desperate that any woman would do rather than wanting you, Davie?"

Remarkably, she laughs, and that has me rolling to my side to see what she thinks is so funny.

"Of all the things I worry about with us, I can honestly say that's not something that ever came to mind."

"Really?"

"Yeah, maybe it's because Jesse is your biological son, so it's not like you would want to replace him. And you've never wanted Jessica. If you really would have accepted anyone in your life just to have somebody, it could have easily been the biological mother of your son, even if she *is* in jail."

"That never would have happened. It's been you from the moment I saw you. There was a visceral reaction I've never had before to anyone else. It's just a bonus that you are my son's aunt."

"Then, we're good," she says, bending lower for a quick kiss, before rearing back with a mischievous smile. "Plus, I like knowing I'm not the only one who gets anxious over random stuff."

"Oh, yeah? Are you making fun of me, wife?" Thankful our conversation didn't turn into the bomb I was afraid it would, I tickle Davie and laugh when she tries swatting me away.

This is how we should spend our time together: laughing then making love. Not concerning ourselves with what others think.

Briggs may be one of my best friends, but he's not number one in my life. Davie and Jesse share that spot.

It would hurt to end our decades-long friendship, but if he can't support me, and be respectful of my family, then that's what will have to happen.

Because I will always protect my wife and son.

# 21

## DAVIE

I'm going to throw up. Somewhere inside the imposing Medford Courthouse is a judge preparing to change the course of the rest of my life.

"Oh, god," I whimper, placing a hand over my knotting stomach.

"Breathe, baby, everything will be alright. I promise."

"You can't promise that," I say, echoing the last time I questioned Cormac when he wanted me to trust him. The thing is, I do trust him. More than I thought would be possible this quickly.

Because this past month has been amazing with the three of us together.

"The tests confirm Jesse is my biological son. You are his biological aunt, and we are legally married. That judge has no choice but to grant us custody. This is just a formality. Isn't that what the lawyer said?"

I nod, too agitated to actually speak.

Jesse babbles from his spot in his stroller. He doesn't have a care in the world. Has no clue of the turmoil his aunt is going through.

"Come here." Cormac pulls me into his arms for a hug, and I can't help but sink into his warmth. Slowly but surely, he's become my safe place.

"Worried, Davie?" Cody's voice breaks into the brief respite.

Jerking to alertness, I try to find my sister's ex, but I'm firmly placed safely behind Cormac as he slowly turns around.

"You must be Cody."

"And who the hell are you?"

"I'm Jesse's dad."

Cody scoffs while his mother skulks in the background. The wild look in her eyes as they ping pong between us and the courthouse steps tells me she may already be high even though it's 11 A.M. in the morning.

"I'm the one Jesse knows as his dad. Jessica thinks this little stunt of digging up a random hookup will steal that kid from me, but I don't think so."

"He's not your *kid*," Cormac growls. "He's mine, and so is his aunt. A woman you won't be tormenting anymore with this bogus custody suit after today."

Cody looks between me and Cormac, a nasty smirk twisting his lips. "I've got to hand it to you, Davie. I didn't peg you for a whore who will spread her legs to receive a welfare check."

"What did you call her?" Cormac takes a threatening step forward, but I cling to the back of his shirt, tugging at the fabric.

"Don't! He's not worth it."

An image of Cormac punching his ex-employee that first day we met flashes in my mind. If Cormac attacks Cody right before we're supposed to meet the judge, no telling what will happen.

"Come on Cody, we don't want to be late." His mom grabs his arm and drags him up the steps, but not before he shoots another sneer our way.

"I don't know how you've dealt with him alone for so long," Cormac says. He twists back around and crushes me to his chest.

His heart pounds beneath my cheek, announcing just how worked up he is over the confrontation. "Trust me, it wasn't easy. Let's hope today's the last we ever see of him."

"It will be." Cormac presses a soft kiss to my lips, then ushers me towards the ramp leading inside, while he pushes Jesse's stroller.

The next hour passes in a haze as we meet my lawyer in the marble hall, get settled in the courtroom, and listen to the judge as he reiterates the DNA results.

When he officially grants Cormac and myself custody, a wave of relief crashes into me so hard I almost black out.

But the relief is short-lived, and not because Cody and his mom start making a fuss, causing the judge to call for the bailiff to control the two.

Jesse's custody is settled, but what does that mean for *my* future?

Cormac and I married for this exact outcome, but what happens next? Do we keep living as we have in a perfect little bubble, like a real family, like a couple in love?

It's far too easy to believe that's what he wants, with each kiss, caress, and talk about watching Jesse grow up together, but it's been a long road to get here.

We've reached the end of one chapter, and Cormac doesn't need me anymore, not as his wife, anyway.

The entire way home to High Ridge and the Rocking M, the thought nags me, along with one very important question.

Does Cormac love me?

Because despite my best intentions, I've fallen for him.

## 22

## CORMAC

The moment we drive under the timber arch displaying the Rocking M name, the familiar sight of Black Mountain rising protectively over the main house and outbuildings, a calm settles over me.

For the first time in months, there's a sense of peace permeating my bones. Not the fleeting kind from the highs of spending time with Jesse and Davie, but long-lasting. A forever kind of contentment knowing my son is legally mine, and so is Davie—no matter how much of a Neanderthal that makes me sound.

The only problem is I'm not sure my wife feels the same peace. She's been quiet on the journey home. Not quite upset, but not exactly happy, either.

Contemplative.

Knowing my wife, she's probably overthinking.

But about what, I don't know.

"Your aunt and I are about to have a serious chat, little man," I whisper to Jesse as I situate him in his crib ten minutes later. "Don't worry, though, your dad plans on fixing whatever is bothering her. I promise."

Davie's already tucked beneath the comforter in her nightgown by the time I enter our bedroom. The glow from her phone casts a blue light on her cheeks as she scrolls up.

Her latest obsession has been reading Hollanov fan fiction to wind down every night, and I can't say I haven't enjoyed the outcome of some of those stories.

They get pretty spicy, and as a result, my wife pounces on my dick like it's a damn lollipop the second I join her in bed.

Not tonight, though.

Tonight, she remains on her side of the mattress, studiously ignoring me while I rest on my side watching her.

"Are we going to talk about what's eating you, sweetheart?" I finally ask after another silent minute.

"What do you mean?"

"Something's been on your mind all day, and I don't think you've made any headway with it in the last twelve hours. Why don't you tell me what's going on? Maybe I can help."

Davie holds her breath for a second then flips her phone down on the nightstand. Her fingers pluck at the bedspread, tension radiating from her body.

"What happens now?" The question is tentative, soft. Like she's afraid of my answer.

Adjusting the hand propped against my cheek, I stare at her in confusion. "Like tomorrow? Or next month? For one thing, we don't worry about losing Jesse anymore."

"No, not about Jesse," she pauses. "Well, I guess it's sort of about him, but mostly, it's about us. What happens now with us?"

"I'm not sure I understand..."

She sighs and sinks further down the bed until we're level with each other. "We married to ensure Jesse stays with us. That's taken care of now, so technically, us *staying* married isn't necessary—"

I whip up and pin Davie to the bed so fast, her sentence cuts off with a shocked blink.

"I know you're not suggesting we get a divorce," I growl, disbelief making the words sound harsher to my ears.

"You could find a woman you love and marry—"

This time it's my mouth stealing the ridiculousness coming from my wife. Like I'd want anyone else after having her.

Breaking the kiss, I draw back enough to meet her dazed eyes. To show her how sincere I am.

"I love you, Davie Madsen. *You.* I thought I made it clear I'm in this for the long haul that morning after our wedding." And every night since with my mouth, hands, and cock.

Davie swallows hard, her chest rising in a deep inhale, pushing her hardened nipples into my pecs. "You love me?"

Hanging my head, I curse her deadbeat parents for making my girl think she'd never have someone in her corner. That she'd never be worthy of love that wasn't based on what she could do for the other person.

I drop a kiss to her sternum. The lace at the edge of her nightgown tickles my lips as I nudge it aside to gently suck her nipple between my lips. Her racing heartbeat picks up speed, her breath becoming short stutters.

"Yes, I love you, sweetheart. You and Jesse are my world," I admit on my way down her generous curves. Her plush breasts. Round belly. Until my shoulders part her thighs, and I can slide my tongue between her damp folds, plunging inside her hot cunt and staying there.

Letting her tight muscles clench and release.

Letting them milk my tongue in desperation as I remain still, just breathing her in and showing her how much she owns me.

"Cormac..." she mewls, rocking her hips upward to try to force a reaction. "I love you, too... I'll love you more if you stop teasing me."

Licking her inner wall, I groan at her sweet flavor before shifting to lap at her clit then rising to notch my cock at her opening.

"Say it again, and maybe I'll fuck you as reminder of how serious I am about this. *Us.*"

Davie's palms cup my bearded cheeks, swiping at the gleam of her arousal edging my lips. "I love you, Cormac Madsen. You broke through my guard walls, no matter how hard I fought to keep them between us. I couldn't help falling for you because you're exactly the kind of man I always fantasized about."

Tears glisten in her eyes as she continues, "Jesse and I fulfill your dreams of a family, but you fulfill my wish for love and security. Even when I told myself you were too good to be true, that we could never be together because of my sister, they were lies to hide my feelings."

"But I can't do that anymore," she admits, and it's with that admission that I reward her with the slow slide of my cock burying deep inside her cunt.

"Thank fuck, baby, because this is the start of our forever. No more drama with courts or exes or doubts. It's you, me, and Jesse."

"You, me, and Jesse," she repeats in awe, a shy smile

gracing her lips before they widen in a gasp as my hips retreat only to plunge forward again.

To where I belong.

With my wife.

My home.

# EPILOGUE
## DAVIE

## *ONE YEAR LATER*

"So, you're doing okay?" I ask for the umpteenth time, and Jessica rolls her eyes, shifting in her chair.

"Yes, I'm fine. I've made friends and joined this group that makes quilts for hospital kids. It gets me out of my cell and keeps me busy."

"Good, good..."

Cormac bumps my shoulder with his. "She likes to worry about the people she loves, but I'm working on helping her relax." He winks at me, causing a blush to bloom on my cheeks.

We've visited Jessica a few times since getting custody of Jesse. The first time Cormac met Jessica again after their one-night stand was awkward for us, but once that hurdle was jumped, things fell into an easy flow.

Jessica likes seeing Jesse, even if she's relieved that Cormac and I are more his parents than she is.

"Good luck." Jessica chuckles, poking my crossed arms on the metal table. "Davie's programmed to be a mother hen—pecking and prodding, concerning herself with every little thing about her chicks."

"Guess it's nice I'll have backup when Linnea moves to High Ridge," Cormac teases with a glint in his eyes.

After months of long-distance, I finally convinced Linnea to ditch the job she hated for one on the Rocking M Ranch as Connor's assistant. His old one retired six weeks ago, and it's been hell searching for a replacement—his words, not mine.

"Damn, everyone's leaving for High Ridge. Maybe I'll head that way once my time's served," Jessica muses.

My expression remains neutral. No way will Jessica survive long in a small town like High Ridge. She enjoys city life too much.

I'm guessing that will be tenfold after being cooped up in prison for a few years.

"You're always welcome for a visit," Cormac says diplomatically, and I hide a smile.

My husband has come a long way since the first time I saw him stomping across the ranch to punch a guy. His temper is rarely seen these days.

Connor says he's mellowed in his old age, but I think it's more of Jesse's influence. Cormac is a wonderful dad. Always careful with his words and actions, so his son emulates the best parts of his dad.

*Just like Cormac did with his father.*

It's sweet seeing them together on the ranch, even though Jesse is still too young to do much more than pet the animals and watch Cormac from the sidelines.

A corrections officer walks up to our table, sidestepping Jesse's stroller where he's been napping for the last half hour.

"Visitation is over. Time to go."

Jessica sighs but stands without complaint. "Thanks for coming to see me." She hugs me then pats Jesse's head. Cormac gets a chin lift in farewell which is fine by him.

"Of course. You're family."

And she inadvertently gave me mine: Jesse and Cormac. For that, I'll always be thankful.

***

**The *Mountain Men of High Ridge* series continues in *Mountain Beast: A Curvy Good Girl/Bad Boy Romance*!**

# THANKS FOR READING
# & DON'T FORGET
# TO RATE/REVIEW!

Please consider leaving a rating/review. Ratings & reviews are the #1 way to support an indie author like me. I appreciate your support!

P.S. Don't miss out on new release news & more HERE!

# ALSO BY HALLIE BENNETT

## STANDALONES

Wood Lessons

Batter Up

## SERIES

Tees & Jeans

Lumberjacks of High Ridge

Curvy College Reunion

Christmas & Curves

Mountain Men of Suitor's Crossing

Heirs of Guardian Valley

Reaper's Wolves Mountain MC

Suitor's Crossing: Hearts Collide

Suitor's Crossing: The Caldwells

Blackchapel Bastards

Mountain Men of High Ridge

# ABOUT THE AUTHOR

Hallie prefers steamy stories where curvy girls are claimed by filthy-talking heroes. And when she ran out of reading material, she decided to write her own stories.

If you want a quick, hot read, she's your girl!